# side
# splitters

'brilliantly chosen by Wendy Cooling ... all are
gripping, and offer real substance ... Each is a ray of
sunshine for parents who are gloomy about the
cost of encouraging their children to read. It's
worth investing in the set.'

# side splitters

stories chosen by
**Wendy Cooling**

Dolphin

A Dolphin Paperback
First published in Great Britain in 1997
by Orion Children's Books
a division of the Orion Publishing Group Ltd
Orion House
5 Upper St Martin's Lane
London WC2H 9EA

Typeset by Deltatype Ltd, Birkenhead, Merseyside
Printed in Great Britain by Clays Ltd, St Ives plc

# Contents

# Smelly Sock Soup

Ruth Symes

I t all began with a poster stuck on the school wall. There was a drawing of a chef's hat on it and underneath was written:

**Willow School Cooking Contest**
All children welcome to enter
Must be able to cook
Heat 1: Soup Stirring
Heat 2: Pie Producing
Heat 3: Dessert Delivering

Harry Jones was reading the poster slowly and thinking that he might, maybe, enter the school Cooking Contest. There were only two entrants so far. They were:

Wanda 'I am a Wondercook' Wiggins

and her twin brother

Wayne 'What a good cook I am' Wiggins.

'What are you looking at that poster for?' Wayne Wiggins asked, poking Harry in the back with a bony finger.

'No point you entering the Cooking Contest Harry,' Wanda Wiggins said. '*You* couldn't even boil an egg without scrambling it.'

'One of us is going to win that Cooking Contest,' said Wayne.

'Our Dad's going to teach us how to make the best Cooking Contest food in the whole world,' said Wanda.

'He's a famous cook,' said Wayne.

'Yeah. He works at the Big Burger Bar,' said Wanda.

'He's going to teach us how to make soups and pies and puddings,' said Wayne.

'And then one of us is going to win the Cooking Contest,' Wanda said.

Wayne and Wanda walked away.

Harry took out a pen and wrote his name beneath Wayne and Wanda's. The Cooking Contest now had three entrants.

When the bell rang for the end of school Harry went home and started cooking.

Choosing what dessert to make was easy. Harry made his favourite, but he had to look in Mum's cookbooks to find a recipe for a soup and a pie.

Mum was very surprised when she came home and found Harry had made the dinner. She liked the tomato soup and she liked the cheese and onion pie, but she didn't want any of Harry's dessert.

So Harry ate it all by himself.

Yum.

'That was very good cooking, Harry,' Mum said.

'Thanks,' said Harry, rubbing his full stomach. 'I've entered the school Cooking Contest. It's on Saturday.'

'Well, I'm pleased you'll be showing off your cooking talents. The tomato soup and cheese and onion pie were delicious,' Mum said.

'I'm glad you liked them,' Harry said, 'because it's only three days to the contest and I'll have to practise ...'

Mum sighed. 'I suppose I can eat tomato soup and cheese and onion pie for the next three days,' she said. 'At least I won't have to cook the dinner. But I don't want any of your special dessert. You can have that all to yourself!'

'I don't mind. I can easily eat a double helping every day,' Harry said.

On Saturday morning Harry set off to school with his soup, pie and dessert ingredients in a large carrier bag.

'Good luck, Harry!' Mum called. She was in the kitchen

making herself something for breakfast that didn't have tomatoes, cheese, onions or pastry in it.

At school Mrs Richards, the head teacher, gave Harry, Wayne and Wanda chef's hats and long white aprons to wear.

Three judges were going to judge the Cooking Contest. They were Mrs Richards, Mrs Greaves, the cookery teacher, and Chef Hotpot.

'Time for the competition to begin,' Mrs Richards said, taking hold of Chef Hotpot's arm, 'Let's go and relax in the staffroom, Chef Hotpot.'

Mrs Greaves sneezed. She had a bad cold but Mrs Richards had said she had to come to the Cooking Contest, because she was the cookery teacher. Mrs Greaves sat at a table in the middle of the cookery room, making sure Harry, Wayne or Wanda didn't cheat or accidentally set fire to the kitchen. 'Dold in my dose,' she grumbled, 'should've stayed in bed.' She rested her head on the table and closed her eyes. 'Dorrible deadache.'

Wayne and Wanda had cooking tables next to each other and Harry was on the end.

Harry carefully chopped his tomatoes and onions, then mixed his soup ingredients together in a saucepan and stirred and seasoned the mixture.

'Harry shouldn't stand a chance!' Wanda whispered to Wayne.

'We can't let him win the competition,' Wayne whispered back.

They glanced over at Harry. He was busily stirring his soup.

'It's not fair!' Wanda whispered.

She looked at Mrs Greaves. Mrs Greaves had fallen asleep!

Now was Wanda's chance to do something about Harry. She ran to the cookery room door, opened it, and said, 'Yes, yes, I'll tell Harry at once.'

Harry heard his name and looked up as Wanda closed the door and returned to her cooking table.

'Harry, Mrs Richards wants to see you straight away,' she said.

'All right,' said Harry.

He turned the heat off his soup and left the cookery room.

Mrs Greaves carried on sleeping.

Mrs Richards wasn't waiting for Harry outside the cookery room, so he went to the staff room to find her.

'I didn't see Mrs Richards,' Wayne said to Wanda.

'Of course you didn't it's a trick,' said Wanda. 'Now's our chance to ruin Harry's soup.'

'Oh ...' said Wayne and he grinned. 'You are clever.'

Wanda smiled. 'What would make you think "yuk!" if you found it in a soup, Wayne?' she asked.

'I'd think yuk if I found a fly in my soup,' said Wayne.

Wanda sighed. 'There aren't any flies in here, Wayne.'

'Or a spider', said Wayne.

Wanda sighed louder. 'Do you see any spiders in here?'

'And an old sock, like the ones I'm wearing, would be disgusting to find in a soup.'

'Don't be si ...' Wanda started to say. But then she stopped and said thoughtfully, 'That might not be a bad idea. That might not be a bad idea at all. That might be the only brilliant idea you've ever had, Wayne.'

'Thanks,' Wayne said.

'Take your sock off then, and drop it into Harry's soup,' Wanda told him.

Wayne pulled off one of his socks and crept over to Harry's soup.

He dropped the sock into Harry's soup, but it didn't sink. It just floated on top of the tomato mixture. Wayne picked up a spoon and pushed the sock down into the soup.

While Wayne was ruining Harry's soup Wanda decided

to ruin Wayne's soup. With Harry and Wayne's soups spoilt she'd be sure to win.

She picked up the salt pot and poured all the salt into Wayne's soup.

Wayne crept back to his table.

'Done it,' he whispered.

Wanda nodded and carried on chopping a beetroot.

Wayne tasted his soup. It tasted … he spat it out. Yuk, it was full of salt!

'Wanda,' he growled. Wanda pretended she hadn't heard him.

Wayne took hold of the pepperpot and tipped all the pepper into Wanda' soup.

'Hey! What're you doing?' Wanda shouted.

Harry walked back into the cookery room. 'Mrs Richards didn't want to see me. She's drinking sherry with Chef Hotpot,' he said.

Mrs Greaves woke up.

'What are you dree doing dalking?' she said, then sneezed and blew her nose. 'Get back to dour places and carry on dooking. You've only got den minutes deft.'

Harry went back to his place, turned the oven back on and stirred his soup. His spoon found something in his soup that shouldn't have been there. A green sock with a hole in it.

Harry was sure socks hadn't been amongst his tomato soup ingredients.

There was only five minutes left to the end of heat one. Not enough time to make more soup. Harry threw the sock away, poured the soup into a large bowl and floated some fresh basil leaves on the top.

Mrs Richards and Chef Hotpot came into the cookery room. Mrs Richards's face looked very red. She clapped her hands. 'Stop cooking. End of heat one!'

Time for the soups to be tasted.

'Well …' said Mrs Greaves when she tasted Wayne's soup.

She couldn't taste much because of her cold, but the soup reminded her of drinking seawater.

'Hm,' said Mrs Richards, pulling a face and forcing herself to swallow rather than spit out Wayne's soup. It tasted horrible.

Chef Hotpot tasted Wayne's soup. His eyes opened wide with horror. 'This soup is revolting. I don't think I've ever tasted anything so foul before,' he said, 'Salty soup is not going to win the competition.'

Mrs Greaves tasted Wanda's soup and sneezed loudly.

Mrs Richards tasted Wanda's soup and choked.

Chef Hotpot tasted Wanda's soup and his eyes almost popped out of his head. 'This is even worse than the salt soup,' he said. 'Peppery soup – hideous!'

Mrs Greaves tasted Harry's soup and thought she tasted a hint of tomato through her cold.

Mrs Richards tasted Harry's soup and sighed with relief.

'I hope your effort is better than Wayne and Wanda's,' Chef Hotpot said.

He dipped his spoon, into Harry's soup, lifted the spoon to his mouth and gingerly sipped it. He looked thoughtful, then dipped his spoon into the soup and tasted it once again.

'This is simply slurpily delicious!' he said and took another spoonful. 'What an unusual tomato soup. It has just a hint of strong cheese.'

'Harry Jones is the winner of heat one,' Mrs Richards announced.

'We have to stop him winning the next heat,' Wayne whispered to Wanda.

'We'll have to do something to ruin his pie,' Wanda whispered back.

'Put something horrible in it?' Wayne asked.

Wanda nodded. 'What do you think would make a pie revolting, Wayne?'

'Worms?' Wayne suggested.

Wanda sighed. 'Do you see any worms in the cookery room?' she asked.

Wayne shook his head. 'Another sock?' he said.

'Didn't work last time, did it?' said Wanda.

'How about a sprinkling of extra hot chilli pepper?' said Wayne, holding up the extra hot chilli pepperpot.

Wanda smiled. 'You should be on *Mastermind*, Wayne,' she said.

'Time for heat two,' said Mrs Richards. She and Chef Hotpot left the cookery room.

Harry, Wanda and Wayne started to make their pies. Mrs Greaves rested her head on the table and went back to sleep.

'Cause a diversion,' Wanda whispered to Wayne.

Wayne quickly obeyed. 'Help, help my saucepan's on fire!' he shouted.

Mrs Greaves woke up fast. Harry and Mrs Greaves went to see what was wrong.

Wanda darted over to Harry's pie mixture and tipped the whole of the pot of extra hot chilli pepper into it. Then she ran back to her place and pretended to be stirring her pie ingredients.

'What a fuss over nothing, Wayne. Your saucepan's not on fire, get on with your pie-making,' Mrs Greaves said.

Harry went back to his place, finished making his pie and put it in the oven.

'Dwo minutes deft,' Mrs Greaves said a while later.

Harry put his oven gloves on and took his pie out of the oven.

Wanda and Wayne put on their oven gloves and took their pies out of the ovens, but they were so busy looking at Harry and not where they were going that they bumped into each other.

'Hey, look out,' said Wayne. But it was too late. His pie went flying through the air.

'No …' shrieked Wanda as her pie flew up to the ceiling and then sank down on to the floor. Splat!

Wayne and Wanda scrambled to pick up the hot pie messes and put them back into the pie tins. Their pies didn't look very tasty.

Mrs Richards and Chef Hotpot came into the kitchen. 'End of heat two,' Mrs Richards said.

'Let's see if your pie-making is better than your soup-making,' Chef Hotpot said to Wayne.

Wayne looked down at his pie. He thought it might taste okay, but it certainly didn't look nice.

Chef Hotpot looked at the mushed pie. 'What's it supposed to be?' he asked.

'Baked bean pie. It tastes lovely. Do you want to try some?' Wayne asked.

'No thank you,' said Chef Hotpot, shuddering at the thought.

Wayne looked at Mrs Richards, who shook her head. 'No thank you Wayne.'

Wayne looked at Mrs Greaves, 'Do dank oo,' she said.

Chef Hotpot looked at Wanda's pie. It looked just as revolting as her brother's had done. A mess of pastry and mush. 'What flavour is this pie supposed to be?' Chef Hotpot asked.

'Cauliflower cheese,' Wanda said.

'Hmm,' said Chef Hotpot, 'I won't try it, thank you.'

'Nor me,' said Mrs Richards.

'Dor dee,' said Mrs Greaves.

The three judges went to see what Harry had managed to make.

Harry's pie at least looked like a pie. Chef Hotpot sighed with relief. 'You've won this round without me even having to taste your pie, Harry. Yours is the only one that even looks like a pie should.'

'Time for heat three,' said Mrs Richards.

Chef Hotpot and Mrs Richards left the room. Mrs Greaves sat back at her table and yawned widely.

'What shall we do to spoil Harry's dessert?' Wayne whispered to Wanda.

'No point doing anything,' Wanda whispered back. 'Harry's won the soup and the pie-making sections and even if we ruined his dessert he'd still have won two out of three heats so he'd be the overall winner.'

'Whatever we do he's won, then?' Wayne asked.

Wanda nodded.

'Might as well just show the judges how good at cooking we really are, then? Wayne said.

'Yeah.'

Wanda and Wayne started to make their desserts. They were both very good cooks – when they weren't trying to ruin someone else's cooking.

Wanda started beating an egg and slicing some plums to make her speciality, plum pancakes.

Wayne started mashing some apricots to make his delicious apricot and orange snow.

They were both too busy making their own desserts to notice what Harry was doing.

Harry happily made his favourite dessert. It smelt delicious. He hoped Chef Hotpot, Mrs Richards and Mrs Greaves didn't eat it all, he hoped they'd leave him some.

The end of the contest soon arrived.

Mrs Richards and Chef Hotpot came into the kitchen. Mrs Richards clapped her hands. 'End of heat three,' she said.

'What have you made this time?' Chef Hotpot asked Wayne.

'This,' said Wayne, showing the chef his perfectly made apricot and orange snow.

'You – you made that?' asked Chef Hotpot in surprise.

Wayne nodded his head.

'It looks almost edible.' Chef Hotpot said, taking a forkful and tasting it.

'Heavenly,' he murmured.

Mrs Richards tasted Wayne's apricot and orange snow. 'Delicious,' she said.

Mrs Greaves tasted it and smiled. She was sure it tasted wonderful but she didn't have any tasting power left.

Chef Hotpot turned to Wanda, 'And what dessert have you made for us?' he asked.

'These,' said Wanda, showing Chef Hotpot her three perfectly made plum pancakes.

'Did you really make those?' Chef Hotpot asked.

'Yes,' said Wanda.

Chef Hotpot tasted one of the plum pancakes. 'Wonderful,' he whispered.

After trying a forkful of plum pancake Mrs Richards asked if she could eat a whole one and Mrs Greaves smiled and nodded her head, although the plum pancakes just tasted pancakeish to her.

Chef Hotpot could hardly wait to see what Harry had made and Harry could hardly wait for the judges to try his dessert.

'What have you made for us Harry?' Chef Hotpot asked.

'This,' Harry said proudly.

Chef Hotpot looked into the dish. He'd never seen anything like it before. Part of it was orange and part of it was green and all of it had lumps sticking out of it.

'What's it called, Harry?' Mrs Richards asked.

'It's my speciality, Mrs Richards. My favourite dessert,' Harry said.

'Yes, but what is it?' Chef Hotpot asked.

'Delicious peach and brussel sprout custard,' said Harry and he held out three spoons for them to taste it.

But Chef Hotpot and Mrs Richards and Mrs Greaves were suddenly not hungry. Even Wayne and Wanda didn't want to taste it.

So Harry was able to eat all of the peach and brussel sprout custard himself.

Yum!

After Harry had eaten every last bit of his dessert, and scraped out the saucepan, it was time for the prizes to be given out.

'Well done, Harry,' said Chef Hotpot, handing Harry the Cooking Contest Champion's prize, a mixing bowl with 'Cooking Champion' engraved on it.

Everyone clapped Harry.

Wayne and Wanda were given joint second prize – a wooden mixing spoon each.

'You'll have to show us how you made that wonderful cheese and tomato flavour soup of yours some time, Harry,' said Mrs Richards.

'Okay,' said Harry. He looked down at Wayne's ankle and the one remaining sock he was wearing. 'If I can get hold of the right ingredients.'

# The Beast of Hawthorne Road

Nick Turnbull

t'll be a disaster!' wailed Mrs Gorrie, wringing her hands and staring at the roof of the assembly hall. 'Just over a week to go and nobody knows their lines.'

The teacher's voice of despair had little effect on George, besides which he was bored. Mrs Gorrie was one of those people for whom life in general was a disaster and listening to her droning on about the school play was just about as interesting as visiting his grandmother. Anyway, he couldn't see why she was making a fuss. The school play was always a shambles, so why should this year be any different?

He turned to Eric, sitting beside him on the bench at the back of the hall.

'The Pilsburys next door have bought a dog.'

'Oh,' said Eric. 'You mean the woman with the blue hair?'

'Yes.'

For some reason best known to herself, Mrs Pilsbury made it her business to visit the hairdresser's every month and have her hair coloured blue. George thought it might be to match the colour of their front door.

'They've had it for three weeks. And it yaps.'

'Most of them do,' said Eric.

'Not all the time.'

'Why not?' said Eric. 'Teachers do.'

He was watching Mrs Gorrie trying to point out to the chorus that if the author of the musical had wanted them to sing 'Food, glorious food, rice pudding and something ... ,' then that's what he would have written.

'Dad says things like that ought to be strangled,' said George.

'What?' said Eric. 'Teachers?'

'No. The dog next door.'

Mrs Gorrie wasn't having much success. Eric wondered why she didn't just give up.

'It'll settle down.'

'No it won't,' said George. 'It's worse now than it was when it first turned up.'

'George! Eric! Will you please stop talking and come down here to the front where I can see you!'

The two boys stood up.

'Bit like Mrs Gorrie, I suppose.'

'Mrs Gorrie says it'll be a disaster,' said George at teatime, sitting at home in number 75 Hawthorne Road and chewing his way through a bowl of what he assumed were lukewarm potato peelings. His mum said it was fish pie and that it had been very easy to make. George wished that his mother would sometimes try something really complicated. Like a sandwich.

'What's it called?'

'*Oliver*,' said George. 'It's about a gang of kids who go around nicking things and singing songs. Only problem is nobody can remember what they're supposed to be singing about.'

'Sounds fun,' said his mum, scrubbing away at the top of the cooker with what looked like the kind of brush that Ernie used to clean out the school toilets.

'It isn't,' said George. 'And has Dad strangled that dog yet?'

George's mum stopped scrubbing for a moment.

'Has he done what?'

'Strangled that dog. He says if the Pilsburys next door don't get rid of it, he'll do it for them.'

'Your dad should be in that musical,' said his mum, turning back to the ever-increasing pile of soapsuds that covered the charred remains of the fish pie. 'They don't know what they're singing about and he doesn't know what he's talking about.'

George had another bite of potato peel and fishbones.

'Best bit's this bloke called Bill Sykes who wanders around with a cudgel saying horrible things to everybody.'

'Who?'

'Bill Sykes. They got Oily Bates to play him. Can't act but he looks ugly enough.'

George watched as his mum hacked away at an especially grisly piece of burnt fish, glued to the side of the cooker.

'I think I might go out in the garden.'

Getting up from the kitchen table, he stuffed what was left of his food into his pocket and headed for the back door.

'Have you had enough, George?'

George nodded, said 'yes' as politely as he could and went out into the small garden at the back of the house.

Scarcely had he done so than the yapping started. A high-pitched, squawking kind of yap. The kind of sound you might expect to hear if you stood on a bad-tempered stoat. And once started, it never seemed to stop until the creature either ran out of breath or was throttled by some well-intentioned passer-by. The dog itself was about the size of a hedgehog and George had loathed it from the moment he'd first clapped eyes on it.

He walked down to the bottom of the garden where there was a hole in the fence.

'Here Trixie! Good girl! Food!'

For a moment, the yapping stopped as the brute heard George's voice and then sniffed the potato peelings which George was now shovelling through the hole. Then, with an especially nasty yap, it turned and bounced down its own garden towards him. George smiled. It hadn't taken him long to discover that one of the few good things about his mother's cooking was that it invariably made the greedy little monster sick.

'I suppose you could always kill it,' said Eric a few nights later, as he and George wandered down Laburnum Road towards the school playing fields.

'With what?' said George.

'Don't know,' said Eric. 'I suppose you need something like a blowpipe and some poisoned darts.'

'Suppose so,' said George, swinging his cricket bat through the air towards an imaginary boundary. 'Haven't got one, have you?'

'No,' said Eric. 'I'm not even allowed a catapult. Can't see why. I mean, my sister's getting a new dolls' house.'

The two boys reached the end of the short road and pulled open the wire gates that led onto the playing fields. Over to the right, five or six kids were playing football. Emma was waiting by the small green hut that Ernie kept the lawnmowers in.

'You're late.'

'Eric was late,' said George.

'I've been trying to learn my words for this stupid play.'

'Can't see why that should make you late,' said Emma, scratching three white chalk lines on the side of the shed. 'You've only got one line.'

'It's quite long,' said Eric. 'And you've got to say it in the right place.'

'Good evening, ladies and gentlemen, and welcome to the school's production of *Oliver*,' said Emma. 'It's a bit difficult to say it in the wrong place.'

'Oh, I don't know,' said George. 'I'm sure Eric will find a way.'

Emma said she was batting first because she'd been waiting so long and took the bat off George, who wandered off to one side of the makeshift cricket pitch as Eric prepared to do his well-known impression of Ian Botham bowling. None of them actually knew who Ian Botham was but Eric's dad said he was the greatest cricketer of all time and had a picture of him in the front hall. Ian Botham might well have been the greatest cricketer of all time but Eric certainly wasn't. When he bowled, he looked like some kind of penguin hopping along an ice floe, whirling both his arms around his head like a helicopter and finally letting go of the tennis ball without any idea at all of where it might end up. As it happened, his first ball flew right over the top of Ernie's shed, his second effort cracked one of the windows and the third bounded four times along the ground before Emma swung the bat at it, just like Indiana Jones killing snakes, and hit it high into the air towards the footballers.

It was George who heard it.

'Oh no.'

Looking round, he could see Mrs Pilsbury and her yapping hedgehog coming through the gates. Emma wasn't a great cricketer either and it wasn't very likely that Eric's dad would ever put her picture up in his front hall but Ian Botham himself would have been proud of the way she had just hit the ball. The only problem was that what goes up must inevitably come down again and if there happened to be a small, noisy creature standing in the way, then that was probably just too bad. It's possible that Mrs Pilsbury could have vaulted into the air and caught the ball with all the grace of a ballet dancer and equally, it's possible that she could have bent over backwards and caught it in her teeth. As it happens, she did nothing and when it finally smacked a somewhat surprised Trixie square between the eyes, she sank to the ground like a sack of potatoes.

'Trixie! Trixie! My darling! The brutes!'

To George's considerable disappointment, the thing appeared to have survived. For a few moments, it lay on its side and twitched and then suddenly jumped up and started hurling itself round and round in circles, yapping as if someone had just stuck a pin in it.

'Sorry,' said Emma, as she ran over towards the irate Mrs Pilsbury and her pet Catherine wheel.

'Sorry? Sorry? You nearly killed him!' screeched the woman.

'It was an accident,' said Emma.

'It was my bowling,' said Eric, as he joined them. 'I'm not very good.'

'Brutes! No wonder there's no telephone boxes left standing with hooligans like you running loose!'

'But we were only ...' said Eric.

'Be quiet! I blame it all on the parents. It's where it all starts, of course.'

'Mrs Pilsbury,' said George. 'Your dog ...'

'And as for you, George, what on earth do you think you're doing? Mixing with ruffians like ...'

'Mrs Pilsbury ...'

'What!'

'Mrs Pilsbury, your dog's just eaten our ball.'

George was looking gloomily down at Trixie who'd managed to stop yapping for just long enough to sink her teeth into the tennis ball and was now happily shredding it.

'Good!' said Mrs Pilsbury. 'Perhaps that'll stop you from trying to kill anyone else.' And she bent down and grabbed the animal by the collar.

'Come on, my little angel. Let's go home to Daddy. And leave that nasty thing alone.'

The dog made a kind of choking noise as Mrs Pilsbury clamped a lead on its collar and jerked it away towards the gate. As George looked down on the chewed remains of his ball, he could hear Trixie yapping all the way back down Laburnum Road.

'Right,' he said. 'That's it.'

However, although Eric, Emma and George spent the next few morning breaks eating chocolate biscuits and talking about poisons, booby-traps and bombs, there didn't seem to be any obvious way of getting rid of Trixie. Eric did come up with a particularly ingenious plan which involved

digging a large hole in the Pilsbury's garden, covering it
with bracken and dock leaves and putting an alligator in
the bottom but the idea was dropped because, as George
pointed out, the alligator would take one bite of Trixie and
almost certainly spit the creature out straight away.

And just to make life really miserable, Mrs Gorrie's
dreadful play was looming. None of the kids could understand why they had to go through with this nonsense every
year.

'It was all right when we were small,' said George. 'Then
you didn't mind getting dressed up as a moonbeam. But
when you're older, it's different.'

'What do you mean?' said Emma, as they sat glumly in
the school hall waiting for Mrs Gorrie to stop blowing her
nose and start the rehearsals.

'Well,' said George. 'How can you expect grown-ups to
take you seriously when they've just seen you prancing
about in short trousers singing about food? And I can't
even sing.'

'It's quite a nice tune,' said Emma.

'Whoever wrote it should have been strangled at birth,'
said George. 'Like that dog.'

'Right, children!'

Mrs Gorrie clapped her hands together and stood up on a
chair. 'I think we should be looking at that scene when Bill
Sykes comes in and ... Good heavens, Bernard. What's
that?'

Bernie Bates, otherwise known as Oily, had appeared at
the hall doorway with a lump of wood in one hand and
what looked like a dog in the other. It was a bit difficult to
be sure at first because it was quite small and seemed to be
covered in some kind of string bag.

'You said as 'ow 'e 'ad a dog, Miss.'

'Who?'

'Bill Sykes. The bloke I'm supposed to be in the play. You

said 'e 'ad a dog.' Oily nodded at the thing under his arm. 'So I brung one.'

Mrs Gorrie looked blankly at Oily.

'Well, I …'

'It's all right,' said Oily. ''e probably won't bite anybody. I fed 'im just before I came out.'

Oily put the dog down on the floor where it stayed quite still, a small pair of black eyes squinting out from under bushy white eyebrows. After a few moments, it began to scratch the wooden floor tiles of the hall and a nasty, low-pitched growling noise began to come from its mouth, almost as if the thing was starting up an engine.

'Do you know what?' said Emma.

'What?' said George.

'That thing looks exactly like that horrible creature that chewed our ball.'

'Maybe it is,' said Eric.

'Don't think so,' said George. 'Anyway, Oily's mum doesn't have blue hair.'

Mrs Gorrie had by now recovered sufficiently to get down off the chair and have a closer look at Oily's dog.

'It's very sweet, Bernard,' she said, putting on her glasses and peering at it. It wasn't very often that Oily showed an interest in anything so she'd decided it was best to encourage him. 'And what do you call it?'

'Please, miss,' said Oily. ''e's called Killer.'

Oily's dog was exactly what they'd been looking for. Not that they realised it at first. In fact, it wasn't until that evening that George had his bright idea.

He was sitting staring out of his bedroom window, an unopened book of French grammar propped upon the small table in front of him, when he saw Mrs Pilsbury pottering about in the garden next door. She was always doing it, which is why it was one of those dreadful, tidy gardens where everything's in a straight line and even the garden gnomes have to keep their boots polished. The lawn was a closely-cropped square of yellow and green where Mrs Pilsbury would sometimes squeeze into a deckchair if the sun was shining. Below the lawn were three rows of rose bushes, then came Mr Pilsbury's small greenhouse and finally, at the bottom of the garden, there were the tangly fruit bushes which hid Trixie from view whenever she stuck her snout through the hole in the fence and scoffed the remains of George's mother's cooking.

George watched as Mrs Pilsbury prodded and poked her way round the edges of the lawn with a small trowel, presumably tidying up any mess left by the odd worm passing by. Trixie was yapping and bouncing up and down on short, stubby legs. Every so often Mrs Pilsbury would call the horrible thing to her and the dog would obediently trot up, hoping for food.

Slowly, the idea began to form in George's mind and slowly he began to smile. And he carried on smiling until his dad stuck his head round the bedroom door and said he'd test him on his French.


Oily wasn't too keen at first. Killer didn't really like strangers but George said that was exactly why he was ideal.

'How much?' said Oily, as the two of them walked slowly round the edge of the school playground during morning break.

'How much what?' said George.

'How much do I get paid?'

'You're not doing anything,' said George.

'But it's my dog,' said Oily, who liked to think he wasn't as daft as he looked.

George thought for a moment or two.

'Twenty pence.'

'Thirty,' said Oily.

'Fifteen,' said George.

'Deal,' said Oily, who'd never been very good with

numbers, and they shook hands as the school bell rang for the end of break.

Eric brought the net. It was actually the cloth bag that his mum used to keep the vegetables in but it was probably a better idea than the biscuit tin George had suggested.

'At least it won't suffocate,' said Eric.

'Pity,' said George.

Glancing through the kitchen window, George's mum could see the kids at the bottom of the garden. Emma and Eric, she knew. But the other one was new to her. George had said he was called Oily but that was probably just George being rude. She had no idea what was in the sack the boy was carrying.

'What's that rabble up to?' said George's dad, coming in through the back door after another exciting day at The Independent Bank Limited.

'You're home late,' said George's mum, turning away from the window as her husband put his battered briefcase on the kitchen table and poured himself a cup of tea. 'You won't be late tomorrow, will you?'

'Why not?'

'Because it's *Oliver*.'

'Who?'

'*Oliver*. The school play.'

'I can't wait,' said George's dad. 'And if that thing keeps me awake again tonight, I'll flatten it.'

Outside, Trixie had just started her yapping for the evening.

'They're coming out,' said Emma, peering over the wooden fence as Mrs Pilsbury appeared at her back door with a watering can.

'So I can hear,' said George.

'How are you going to get its attention?' said Eric, crouching down behind the fence beside George and Oily.

'Simple,' said George, sticking his hand in his pocket and pulling out a fistful of crumbling sludge. 'It's one of Mum's chocolate cakes. One sniff of this lot and the little brute will be down here before you can say tummy-ache.'

'Smells quite nice,' said Oily.

'You're right, George,' said Emma, still peering over the fence. 'It's coming.'

Sure enough, Trixie's nose had started twitching in the air and she was now padding through the roses and past the greenhouse towards the fruit bushes.

'Ready?' said George.

'Ready,' said Eric.

And as Trixie followed the smell through the fruit bushes and finally stuck her head through the hole in the fence to gobble up the evil-smelling cake, she was surprised to find herself being grabbed by the scruff of the neck and pushed into a cloth bag.

'How do we stop it yapping?' said Eric.

'Give it some cake,' said George. 'Right, Oily. This is where you earn your fifteen pence.'

Oily grinned and reached into his sack.

By now, Mrs Pilsbury had noticed that her little bundle of joy seemed to have gone missing.

'Trixie! Trixie! Where are you? Come along, poppet. Mummy's got some nice biccies for you.'

'What's a biccy?' said Emma.

'Some people are like that,' said George. 'They seem to think that if they talk rubbish, animals understand them.'

Mrs Pilsbury was standing on her lawn, still hanging on to her watering can and looking down the garden. Then she smiled as she saw a movement in the fruit bushes.

'Aha. Mummy can see you, you naughty little scallywag. Yes she can. Mummy can see you.'

And she started walking down the short path that ran down the centre of the garden. 'Come on, darling. Biccies.'

When she reached the bushes, she stopped, peering in through the tangle of spiky branches.

'Ah. There you are, diddums,' she said after a few moments, spotting a small white furry shape among the bushes. 'Come on, darling. We've got to put some warty-water on the lawney-worney.'

There was a low growling sound from the bushes.

'Trixie?'

Moments later, Killer burst out of the gooseberries, snapping and snarling like an ill-tempered warthog, and sank his teeth into Mrs Pilsbury's plastic watering can. With a shriek, she dropped it and, with the kind of look on her face she might have had if she'd just come across Tyranno-saurus Rex, the poor woman ran screaming back up the garden path with Killer snapping and barking at her ankles and every so often grabbing a mouthful of her billowing skirt.

'You foul creature! Beast! Horrid animal! Help! Aaargh!'

With one last piercing shriek, Mrs Pilsbury cleared the lawn in one leap. Throwing herself through the back door, she slammed it shut behind her, leaving Killer to jump up and down against it, scratching the wood and barking like a werewolf. If the dog had known what a phone was, he'd have heard Mrs Pilsbury grabbing the one in the kitchen, dialling 999 and screaming down the receiver that she'd been set upon by a pack of wolves. As it was, Killer soon got bored and after barking nastily three or four times, he turned and scuffled back down the garden, stopping only for a final chew on the watering can.

'C'm'ere,' hissed Oily through the hole in the fence.

Since Oily was the only person who ever fed him, Killer generally did what Oily wanted. Crawling back through the bushes, he let his owner pick him up and put him back in the sack.

'Do we let it go again now?' said Eric.

'Why not?' said George and they unfastened the vegetable bag, letting Trixie have one last bite of chocolate cake before pushing her back through the fence.

'Right,' said Oily. 'Fifteen pence.'

'Worth every penny,' said George.

When the police eventually did turn up, they weren't too impressed with Mrs Pilsbury's rantings about wolves. On the back lawn, they found a small white dog that yapped a lot and looked as if it was going to be sick but otherwise seemed perfectly harmless.

Sitting in his garden, George could hear Mrs Pilsbury screaming about demons, fangs and rabies and that she was never going to have another animal and that she couldn't understand why her husband had ever bought this brute in the first place. And later, George saw Mr Pilsbury appear with a large cardboard box which, very carefully, he put on top of Trixie.

'Perhaps we should take her back to the shop, dear,' George heard him call to his wife.

'The shop!' she screamed. 'What's wrong with the zoo?'

A window slammed and for the first evening in three weeks peace returned to 75 Hawthorne Road.

Mrs Gorrie was wrong. Far from being a disaster, *Oliver*, as performed by the kids of Houghton Primary, was one of the funniest things their parents had ever seen. Even George's dad said he'd have happily paid money for a ticket.

Nobody knew their lines. That went without saying. Even Eric, as George had quite rightly predicted, managed to walk onto the stage and say Good Morning instead of Good Evening. But from the moment Oily's dog appeared, the performance became one of those occasions that nobody would ever forget, even if, perhaps, Mrs Gorrie wanted to.

Somehow or another, Killer managed to break free from Oily's lead and then spent the rest of the play terrifying anybody unlucky enough to start singing. Billy Jenkins, starring as Fagin, got half way through some ditty about picking a pocket or two when a nasty snap at his right ankle sent him scrambling up the curtains at the side of the stage. Sally Blenkinsop, as Nancy, would have completed a heartrending version of 'As Long As He Needs Me' if she hadn't run shrieking off the stage, chased by a none-too-tuneful Killer, and when Tom Froggitt, as Oliver, stuck his hands in the air and sang 'Who Will Buy This Beautiful Morning?', Eric's dad fell off his chair laughing, saying he wasn't too keen on the morning but he'd give five pounds for the dog. All the while, Oily ran round and round the stage, saying some very rude things and shouting abuse at his dog, and everyone agreed that it was one of the best performances of Bill Sykes they'd ever seen.

And it might have gone on for the entire evening if Killer hadn't finally jumped up on top of Mrs Wilkinson's piano and snarled at her. Having bravely battled on through the chaos, the sudden appearance of Oily's pet, inches from her nose, was too much for the old dear who screeched and bolted for the safety of the staffroom, her sheets of music scattering across the wooden floor like confetti.

Needless to say, it was all over a little earlier than expected and it was still light as George and his parents walked back home down Hawthorne Road. As they neared their house, George was just wondering whether or not there might be time to go round to Eric's house when, to his surprise and then to his horror, he saw something moving under the laurel bush in the small garden at the front of the Pilsbury's house.

'Oh no,' he muttered. 'I don't believe it.'

As they passed the gate, George stopped and, bending down, peered through the wrought iron loops of the front gate. As he did so, the small shadow he'd seen moving ambled towards him, purring. George smiled.

'Don't tell me. They've called you Kitty Witty.'

'Pussykins! Pussykins!'

Mrs Pilsbury's voice could be clearly heard round at the back of the house.

'Mumsy's calling!'

The small cat hissed at the sound and crept back into the shadows of the laurel bush. George straighted up again and smiled.

He didn't think they'd need to borrow Oily's cat.

# Always Smile at the Clockodile

Ann Jungman

As soon as she got home from school Annie did what she always did. She put on her wellington boots and went to play in the stream that ran along the bottom of her garden. At first it was like any other day but then the most unexpected thing happened. A crocodile put his head out of the water and with a big smile on his face said:

'Good afternoon, little girl.'

Annie stared at the crocodile in horror and said nothing.

'I said "Good Afternoon little girl",' repeated the crocodile. 'And it would be polite if you were to smile and say "Good afternoon" back.'

'I know better than that,' replied Annie. 'I know that you never smile at a crocodile.'

'That is absolutely correct, but you see I am not a crocodile.'

'You don't fool me,' cried Annie. 'If you're not a crocodile what are you?'

'I'm a clockodile. Look! See, I've got a wonderful big clock on my back. Come closer, you'll see.'

Annie thought the crocodile was trying to trick her to come close enough for him to eat her, so she climbed a tree and crawled down a branch. There, to her surprise, she saw that there really was a clock on the creature's back.

'See, I really am a clockodile. Now will you smile and say "Good afternoon"?'

'What's the difference between a crocodile and a clockodile?' asked Annie, 'Apart from the clock on the back, that is?'

'Oh all the difference in the world,' the clockodile assured her. 'You see us clockodiles are very rare. We are gentle and loving, and what we like most of all in the whole world is to help people.'

'Help people?' cried Annie in amazement.

'Yes, that's it. We always like to help people be punctual and on time. Anyone who owns a clockodile is a very lucky person. Now will you smile and say "Good afternoon", because you always smile at a clockodile.

'What I remember,' objected Annie, 'was that the song went "Never smile at a crocodile, No you can't get friendly with a crocodile".'

'Quite so,' agreed her friend. 'But I am a clockodile, so you can forget all that stuff.'

Annie gave a big smile and said, 'Good afternoon, Clockodile.'

'At last!' shrieked the clockodile. 'Now, little girl, will you introduce me to your mother. We must tell her that she is a lucky person because you now own a clockodile.'

So Annie tied her scarf round the clockodile's big jaw and holding hands they walked up the garden towards the kitchen.

'Take your boots off and leave them outside,' called Annie's mum.

'Yes Mum,' Annie replied. 'And I've brought a friend home.'

'Good,' said Mum. 'What would your friend like for tea?'

'What would you like for tea?' Annie asked the clockodile.

'Mmmmmmm,' mumbled the clockodile through Annie's scarf.

'It's not an ordinary kind of friend,' Annie told her mum, 'it's a clockodile.'

'A what?' demanded Mum and then she turned and saw the clockodile standing in the kitchen door. Mum screamed as loud as she could.

'It's all right,' Annie assured her, 'it's not a crocodile, he's a clockodile.'

'A clockodile!' said her mum. 'Well, don't just stand there, take that silly scarf off his nose.'

'Madame,' said the clockodile, as the scarf was removed, 'it is an honour and pleasure to be in your house.'

'It is an honour and a pleasure to have you here,' said Mum. 'And very useful as well. No one in this house ever manages to be on time for anything. Annie's always late for school, my husband is always late for work, I never make it on time for any appointment and we always miss the beginning of the news. You are very welcome here.'

'So you know about clockodiles then?' said Annie, a bit surprised.

'Oh yes,' said Mum, 'but I never, ever thought I'd meet one, you are so very rare. I certainly never imagined I'd have one in my house.'

'How did you hear about clockodiles?' demanded Annie.

'Well, my Great-Aunt Mildred, who was one hundred and four at the time, told me about a clockodile she had met in India, when she was just a little girl.'

'In India,' said the clockodile dreamily. 'Ah yes, that must have been my Great Uncle Ferdinand. He spent some time in India. What a small world.'

'What's your name?' Mum asked the clockodile.

'Oh, you can just call me Clockodile,' he replied. 'It is so unlikely that another clockodile will ever come this way that I think it would be quite safe.'

'Does Dad know about clockodiles too?' asked Annie.

'I doubt it,' sighed her mother, 'but we'll just have to cross that bridge when we come to it.'

Annie and her mum and Clockodile all sat round the kitchen table and drank tea and ate cakes and chatted happily. Then they heard Dad's key in the door.

'Hello there,' called Dad. 'I'm home. What's for supper?'

'You're cooking tonight,' Mum called back. 'You said you'd make a cheese soufflé.'

'So I did, so I did,' said Dad as he walked into the kitchen. 'I bought the eggs yesterday and ...'

He stopped in mid-sentence, as he caught sight of Clockodile.

'Help!' he shrieked and rushed upstairs. 'Don't worry you two, stay calm, I'll call the police.'

Mum and Annie raced after him.'

'No, Dad!' yelled Annie. 'He's a friend, he's harmless and he's very, very, lucky.'

'Yes, Allan,' said Mum. 'He's not a crocodile, really not. He's a clockodile. Remember I told you about Great-Aunt Mildred's pet? Well, it's one of those. He's really very nice indeed.'

'Are you absolutely sure?' demanded Dad, as he came slowly downstairs, holding his cricket bat above his head. 'Because if he's not I'll thump him.'

'Please, put down that cricket bat and have no fear for your safety or that of your family. Let me help you in the preparation of the soufflé. Timing is so very important in the preparation of that dish.'

'We'll try it,' said Dad grudgingly. 'But if you get up to any tricks you'll regret it. I'm very fierce with a cricket bat.'

But Clockodile behaved beautifully. Just before supper was ready he helped Annie lay the table and told Mum to prepare the salad. Then he handed Dad the oven glove and shouted:

'Now – it will be done to perfection.'

Dad flung open the oven, picked up the soufflé and placed it in the centre of the table. All four of them tucked in and declared it to be the best soufflé ever. Dad glowed at all the praise.

'Well, it was Clockodile really. His timing was just right.'

'Of course,' said Clockodile, wiping his mouth. 'That is what I am here for. Now, turn on the television. It's time for the news.'

When it was time to go to bed Mum asked Clockodile where he would like to sleep.

'Clockodiles always sleep in the middle of the mantelpiece,' he told her, 'just in case someone needs to know the time in the middle of the night. Also, of course, that is where the most elegant clocks are always placed and I regard myself as a very elegant clock indeed.'

So Mum moved all the ornaments on the mantelpiece and Clockodile climbed up and spread himself out and fell asleep in a second.

The next morning at seven o'clock Mum and Dad were woken by a knock on the door.

'Come in,' mumbled Mum sleepily.

In waltzed Clockodile with a tray of tea.

'Come on, up you get,' cried Clockodile. 'Drink up your tea quickly. Then Dad go and shave, while Mum and I go for a run round the block. Breakfast is all ready downstairs. I'll wake Annie up on my way downstairs.'

Mum gulped down her tea while she put on her tracksuit. Soon she and Clockodile were running along.

'I know you want to improve your performance,' he said, 'so I'll time you and we'll try and get it a minute or two faster every day.'

As soon as they got home Mum went off to have a shower and Clockodile served breakfast to Annie and Dad. Then he gave Dad his briefcase and the daily paper and said:

'Now off you go or you'll miss your train and be late again.' Dad was so surprised he called 'Goodbye' to Mum and Annie and disappeared. Annie turned on the television.

'No you don't' said Clockodile firmly. 'You go and clean your teeth and I'll prepare your lunch box and then I'm taking you to school. Can't have you being late. Your mum'll never be out of the shower in time to take you.'

So a few minutes later Annie and Clockodile were walking to school. Clockodile noticed that the church clock was five minutes slow. 'No wonder people are always being late,' he muttered to himself.

At the school gate Clockodile said:

'See you later alligator.'

'In a while clockodile,' replied Annie, grinning.

Clockodile handed Annie her lunch box, gave her a kiss and waved to her as she went into school. All the other children and the parents rushed for cover. The teacher blew the whistle, screamed and ran inside.

'Don't worry, they'll get used to me in no time,' said Clockodile cheerfully, as he set off home to do the washing up.

But Clockodile was wrong. That evening as the family sat round eating supper they heard the sound of shouting and tramping. It seemed to be coming nearer.

They began to be able to hear what the shouts were: 'Crocodiles out' and 'Crocodiles are a danger to the community' and 'Take him to the zoo' and 'Block the Croc'.

Big tears ran down Clockodile's cheeks.

'They don't want me here,' he wept. 'They think I am a dangerous crocodile.'

Annie flung her arms round him.

'Don't worry, we'll look after you.'

'Yes,' agreed Dad. 'But I think you may have to go away for a little while, Clockodile, 'while we prove how nice and helpful you are and what a useful member of society.'

The shouting got louder and looking out of the window, Annie saw a huge crowd with a banner demanding the crocodile be taken away immediately. A large police van drew up and four policemen with guns jumped out.

'There are police there with guns,' she whispered.

'Don't worry,' said Clockodile, drying his tears. 'No point in weeping clockodile tears. Go and tell them that I am coming peacefully. I'll soon convince them that I'm harmless. I'll be back in no time.'

The door bell rang loudly and they heard a shout of 'Open in the name of the law!'

Clockodile stood up very straight and walked to the door with Dad on one side and Annie on the other.

'Here we go,' he said bravely, as Mum opened the door.

Outside the door stood the four armed policemen and behind them an angry crowd shouting, 'Crocs out crocs out, out, out, out!'

'Madam,' said the policeman, 'we understand you have a dangerous crocodile in this house.'

'Not at all,' interrupted Clockodile. 'There is a mistake, officer, I am a clockodile, as you can see from the clock …

But Clockodile was not allowed to finish his sentence. Two policemen rushed in and tied up his big jaw with rope.

'You'll hurt him!' cried Annie.

'Hurt him! He'd hurt us, more like. You were very foolish to have a crocodile in the house. You're all lucky to be alive.'

'But officer, he isn't a crocodile, he's a clockodile, look at the clock on his back. He's not only harmless, he's positively useful.'

'Mmmmmm!' nodded Clockodile energetically.

'That's as maybe,' pronounced the officer. 'But the whole neighbourhood has been terrorised by the rumour that there was a crocodile loose around the place and my orders are to take him in. We've got a big tub in the van outside, he can swim around in there. And we've got an expert from the zoo to look after him.'

'He doesn't need water,' explained Annie …

'Look,' said Dad. 'You take him and we'll come down to the police station. I'll bring my encyclopaedia, which tells you everything you need to know about clockodiles.'

Clockodile was marched out of the house and into the van. The crowds in the street cheered.

'Must be mad keeping a crocodile in the house. Need their heads read.'

'Yeah, and good riddance to the beast.'

'Take him away, we don't want that kind of thing round here.'

Clockodile climbed into the van and waved sadly at Annie and Mum and Dad, as the doors slammed on him and were firmly locked.

Dad grabbed two encyclopaedias and they all got into the car and drove as fast as they could to the police station. When they got there they found Clockodile in a cell and with handcuffs on, but his jaw was not tied up any more. He was busy explaining to the police officer about clockodiles and how they were very rare and could talk and only wanted to help people.

'Well, I don't know what to do,' moaned the police officer. 'I've never had to deal with anything like this, and I don't know what to make of it.'

'Now you know he's no danger, can he come home with us?' asked Annie.

'Can't do that,' explained the police officer. 'I mean, we'd never get a minute's peace, people on the phone every five minutes complaining abut this crocodile on the loose. If we explained he was a clockodile and no problem, they'd think we'd gone daft. I've rung for a famous professor, an expert on crocodiles, and come and give us advice.'

A few minutes later the professor ran into the police station.

'The clockodile, where is it? What an opportunity, what a break, I've always wanted to see one.'

'Over here,' cried Clockodile. 'I'm very happy to see you.'

'Well, this is something, I've been looking for a clockodile all of my life,' said the professor, shaking hands with Clockodile.

'Please tell the police it's safe for us to take him home,' said Annie.

'To be perfectly honest with you, I don't think it would be. All kinds of dreadful things might happen to him if he were not protected. He might be shot, or poisoned, or fall into a trap. I think for the time being he will have to be somewhere protected,' said the professor.

'Like where?' asked Clockodile.

'I think you should live in the zoo for a while. We will have a special Clockodile House and people can come and look at you and talk to you. That way you would get known but the general public would feel safe. I myself would like to study you in that period.'

'It might be lonely and boring,' sniffed Clockodile. 'And I wouldn't be able to help people be punctual.'

'Oh, I think we could find a way round that,' said the professor. 'You could make sure all the animals were fed on time and that the zoo opened and closed on the dot.'

'I suppose I shall have to agree,' said Clockodile with a sigh. 'But I hate the idea of a zoo. Please try and make it for as short a time as possible.'

Clockodile was transferred to the zoo, where he had his own quarters. He quickly became friendly with the zoo-keepers and they came and played chess and cards with him. Soon Clockodile was going with the keepers on their rounds to feed and clean the animals. The zoo had never been so efficient.

Clockodile himself was a big attraction. There were articles in the newspapers and television programmes about him and soon Clockodile was drawing bigger crowds than all the other animals put together. He would stand in his cage and talk to his admirers and pose for photographs. After a while he began to give a tea party for children. It always started on the dot of three and finished at twenty minutes to four. Some days Clockodile would give children rides on his back. He was so popular, that everyone smiled at the Clockodile.

Several times a week Annie would come and visit Clockodile.

'It's all right here,' he would tell her. 'Everyone is very nice to me, but I would much rather be back at home with you. The professor has nearly completed his study and everyone knows I'm harmless now.'

'We want you to come home too,' Annie told him. 'But the police and people still think you might cause riots and things if you were free.'

'Oh dear,' sighed Clockodile. 'Why are people so silly?'

But then something happened that was to change Clockodile's life. Big Ben broke down. Big Ben is the enormous clock just by the Houses of Parliament in the middle of London and the whole country set their clocks and watches by it. Some very important people came to the zoo to ask Clockodile if he would stand at the top of the tower and pretend to be Big Ben until the clock was mended.

'Of course!' cried Clockodile. 'Of course I will. There is nothing in the world a clockodile likes so much as to help human beings to be punctual. But only on one condition.'

'Anything,' agreed the important people, 'If you will help us out in this crisis. Name your price, we will give money or a splendid home, a knighthood, anything you want.'

'All I want is to go back home and live with Annie and her family,' Clockodile told them.

'Done,' cried the important men.

So Clockodile was put high up on Big Ben by a crane. Every hour he could be heard making the sound of the big clock. If it was four o'clock, Clockodile would go:

'Dong, dong, dong, dong!'

If it was ten o'clock Clockodile would go:

'Dong, dong, dong, dong, dong, dong, dong, dong, dong, dong.'

Then all over the country people would hear the sound and put their own clocks and watches right.

Clockodile became quite a national hero. There were pictures in every paper of him standing by Big Ben. By the time the clock was mended there wasn't anyone in the whole country who hadn't heard of Clockodile.

As Clockodile was lowered from the high tower there was a big crowd cheering. The Prime Minister waited at the bottom to congratulate Clockodile and thank him and tell him that there was now no reason why he should not go home with Annie and her family.

'I shall do that, sir,' said Clockodile. 'And if there is anything more I can do to help the nation do not hesitate to call on me. As you know, there is nothing clockodiles like better than being helpful to people.'

No sooner had Clockodile arrived home than the phone started to ring. His services were in demand everywhere. First of all the local hospital were very keen to have Clockodile come in daily and persuade the children to take their medicine on time.

'Certainly,' said Clockodile, 'I'll be on duty at 5.30 a.m.'

The next phone call was from Annie's school. They wanted some help with teaching the children how to tell the time.

'No problem,' Clockodile assured them. 'I'll be in at 10.30 on the dot. By that time I should have finished with the morning shift at the hospital.'

They were just sitting down to a supper to celebrate Clockodile's return home when the phone rang again.

'It's for you, Clockodile,' said Dad.

'Tell whoever it is that I'm about to sit down for my supper, but I will call them back at three minutes past nine exactly.'

'Right,' said Dad. 'Now, I'm doing steaks for supper. How well do you like yours done, Clockodile?'

'Medium rare please,' said Clockodile.

'Good,' said Dad. 'I like mine rare, Mum likes hers medium and Annie likes hers well done.'

'I will time the cooking so that we all get our steak exactly as we like it,' said Clockodile.

Clockodile did as he had promised and they all agreed that they had never eaten such a delicious steak. Just as they were finishing their coffee, Clockodile announced that it was two and a half minutes past nine and made his phone call.

'Good evening, Clockodile here, I understand you wished to speak to me. Time the races? Yes, certainly, it will be a pleasure. Just let me know where and when and I'll be there.'

He turned to Mum and Dad. 'That was the local athletics association. They want me to be their timekeeper. Oh my goodness, I shall be busy. Just the way clockodiles like it. Now, Annie, it's three and three quarter minutes after your bedtime. Off with you!'

'Very well.'

Annie gave him a big hug and a kiss.

'It's so nice to have you back,' she told him.

Just then the phone rang again.

'You answer it,' said Mum. 'It's bound to be for you.'

'Good evening, Clockodile speaking. Ah television, how can I help you? Split second programme timing, I see. Well, I don't see any problem with that. Just let me consult my diary. Yes, I will be free two evenings a week between six and eight. I'm very sorry, but at the moment that is the best I can do. You see, I am in great demand in hospitals and schools and athletic clubs, but I will try and find some more time for you. Good, so I'll expect the car tomorrow at 5.15 p.m. on the dot.'

'What was that?' asked Dad.

'The television people are having some problems getting their programmes the right length, so I'm going to help them,' said Clockodile.

'We'll never see you,' moaned Mum. 'Annie will be so disappointed and so will I. After all the trouble it took to get you back!'

Clockodile kissed her hand.

'It's very nice of you to say so, but the public interest comes first with clockodiles. But I promise to be here at seven o'clock in the morning to bring you tea in bed, have breakfast with you and get Dad off to work and Annie off to school.'

From then on Clockodile hardly had a free moment. At the crack of dawn he was persuading children to take medicine. Then he dashed home for breakfast. Then he did a round of the schools helping children to learn to tell the time. Then he would go off to the athletic stadium and time all the activities; the running and the jumping and the hurdling. Two evenings a week he went to the television studios to help with the programme timing and on Saturdays he was the timekeeper for the local football team. Everyone agreed that Clockodile was a wonderful and helpful creature. Then one day a very official envelope arrived addressed to Mr Clockodile.

'Open it,' said Annie. 'It looks really exciting.'

Clockodile opened the envelope.

'It's from the British Olympic Committee,' he told them with a big grin. 'They want me to be the official timekeeper for the Olympic Team.'

'You'll do it, of course?' said Dad.

'Of course,' agreed Clockodile. 'I have to time all the running and the jumping and the swimming and the horse racing and the skiing events. Oh, I shall be useful!'

Clockodile wrote a very polite letter accepting the invitation, but only on condition that Annie and her mum and dad could come with him. The Olympic Committee were delighted.

When the time came they all flew out with the Olympic team, who cheered Clockodile as he got on the plane.

When it was time for the opening ceremony all the teams had to march round the Olympic Stadium. The athletes voted that Clockodile walk in front carrying the flag. When it was the turn of the British contingent out marched Clockodile wearing the British cap and blazer and holding the flag high up in front of him. A gasp went up from the crowd. They had never seen anything like it. Then when they realised who it was they all stood up and waved and everyone smiled at the Clockodile.

# Spider George

Alex Shearer

S pider George had a bad dream, and so he woke and shouted for his mother.

'Mum, Mum!' he yelled. 'Help, come quick!'

'What is it, dear?' she said. 'Whatever is the matter?'

'Help,' said George. 'I'm frightened! There's a person in the room!'

'Oh, George,' his mother said. 'Not that again. Don't be so silly!'

'No, there is,' said George. 'There really is!'

His mother looked around the room but could not see anyone.

'Look under the chair!' George said.

She did, but could see nothing.

'It was just a dream, George, that was all.'

'It wasn't,' said George. 'I saw them! It was a nasty person. One of the horrible ones. You know – with two legs!'

'Oh, George,' his mother said. 'You're imagining it.'

'I'm not,' George said. 'It was coming to get me! Can I come and sleep in your web?'

'Well, try to get back to sleep in your own room first, George. You know when you sleep in our web that you only keep your father awake, snoring and kicking him in the back. Here, I'll tuck you in.'

So George's mother tucked him back into his web, which wasn't easy, as he had eight legs. And as soon as she got five or six of them tucked in, two or three of them would drop out. But she managed it in the end, and she put on his night-light, and at last he got back to sleep.

At breakfast next morning, George's mum said to his father:

'We're going to have to do something about George. He's frightened of people. In fact, he's got quite a phobia about them.'

'Oh, I wouldn't worry too much,' George's father said. 'He'll grow out of it. When I was his age, I used to be quite frightened of people myself. But they don't bother me now. I still don't like the really big nasty ones, but the little ones are perfectly harmless, and can even be quite useful. They're good at putting the rubbish out, and things like that.'

But no sooner had he finished speaking then there was a terrible cry, and a second later, George ran in, in a terrible state of agitation.

'Help, help,' he yelled. 'I went to use the loo, but there's a person under the toilet seat!'

'Oh, George,' his mum said. 'You're imagining it.'

'I'm not,' said George. 'There's a person in the toilet bowl. Maybe even two of them. With big teeth. Waiting to bite me on the bottom.'

'Come along, George,' his mother said. 'I'll go with you.'

And she went with him and showed him that there were no people there at all.

George played happily by himself for the rest of the morning. His mother took him to the park in the afternoon, where he practised his silk spinning among the trees. After that, he played hide and seek and musical webs with his friends, then they went home for tea.

George's mother was in the kitchen taking a packet of frozen flies out of the freezer, when she heard another scream, this time from the bathroom.

She ran there at once.

'What is it George?' she said. 'Whatever is the matter?'

'Look,' George said. 'Look, look! There's a person in the bath! They must have come up the plughole.'

'Honestly, George, there's no one there.'

'There is!' George cried. 'They've gone now, but there *was* someone. They've gone back down the plughole, that's all.

They're waiting to get me at bath time. They live down the plughole and they wait until a poor spider comes by, then they pop up and grab you. And they hit you with a newspaper. Or they pull all your legs off, just for fun.'

'Stuff and nonsense,' his mother said. 'People don't do things like that.'

'They do!' George said. 'They do! Quick, pour a kettle of hot water down the plughole and make the horrible people go away.'

'All right, maybe a few people do nasty things, the ones who don't know any better. But that doesn't mean that *all* people are nasty. I mean, some spiders are nasty too, George. But we're not, are we? We don't go crawling up people's trouser legs and frightening them, do we?'

'No – I suppose not,' George agreed.

'Just try not to think about it,' his mum said.

'I'll try,' George said.

But it wasn't easy. It wasn't easy *not* to think of something at all. For the more you tried not to think of it, the more you did.

When George's dad came home from his web-building business, George's mum told him what had happened that afternoon, and he decided it was time that he and George had a talk.

'Tell me what the problem is, George,' he said. 'What is it you don't like about people? Why do they frighten you so much, do you think?'

'Well, first, it's their legs,' George said. 'They've only got two, dad! They look so strange and creepy they give me the shudders.'

'But George,' his dad said, 'not everyone has eight legs like us, you know. Why, ladybirds, they only have six legs. And cats, they just have four. And a snail I saw this morning, why, she only had a foot, and the worm that she was talking to had simply no legs at all. And then, on the other side of the coin, there's a millipede out in the garden

..................................................................................

who has so many legs, he can't even count them all. Because by the time he's counted the ones he's got, he's gone and grown some new ones.'

'Yes, I suppose so,' George said. 'But it's not just that, Dad.'

'What else then?'

'Well, their legs aren't properly hairy. Not like ours. Not like yours and mine and Mum's. Why, Mum's got really nice hairy legs. And it's what they eat too.'

'What people eat, you mean?'

'Yes,' said George. 'They don't eat proper food, do they, not like flies. They have things like chips and fish fingers! Eeeech! I mean, just imagine it, Dad, fish fingers. It's enough to make you ill.'

'Yes, I can see what you're getting at, George, and I take your point,' his dad said. 'But you have to remember that different creatures like to eat different things. And it would never do if we all ate the same food, as there might not be enough to go round. Why, if people lived on flies, the same as we do, they'd scoff the lot and we'd have none. But I agree with you that chips do sound disgusting, and there's nothing I like better myself than a big juicy fly. Flies for breakfast, gnats for tea, and a nice bluebottle sandwich in my lunch box, with a daddy longlegs for afters. But we have to live and let live. And though fish fingers and chips might seem strange to us, to other creatures, nothing could be nicer.'

'Yes, Dad, but –' George tried to say, but it was hard to get a word in once his dad had got going.

'Why, a dog I knew once,' Dad went on, 'when I used to have a web out by the water barrel – I was a single spider in those days, this was before I met your mother – why that dog he liked nothing better than a bone. And a sheep of my acquaintance, she was very fond of grass. Now grass isn't my cup of tea, in fact, I don't like cups of tea at all. I much prefer a dew drop, or a spot of rain on a leaf. And –'

......................................................................

'Yes, I know, Dad,' George said. 'But it's not just that, it's the way people stand on the *floor*, instead of living half way up the wall, or dangling from the ceiling, like they ought to. They just don't know how to behave or have any manners at all.'

'Hmm, maybe so,' Dad said. 'But what you have to remember is that often, people are just as afraid of spiders as spiders are of people.'

'Yes, Dad,' George said. 'If you say so.' But he didn't really believe it.

Because how could a person be afraid of a spider? People were huge, and spiders were tiny, even the biggest of them was nowhere the size of a person. People couldn't be afraid of spiders, could they? Especially of ones as small as George, who wasn't even big enough yet to catch flies.

It was ridiculous. He couldn't believe that.

But that night, George woke again with the horrors, and his mum had to go and comfort him.

'There's a person in the wardrobe!' he said. 'And it's coming to get me!'

'Oh, George,' his mum said, opening up the wardrobe door, so that he could see there was nothing there. 'What are we going to do with you!'

And it was ages before he could get back to sleep. His mum had to stay with him, singing him spider lullabyes called Spiderbyes, and telling him his favourite stories, such as Spider In Boots, Rumple-spider-skin, The Spider and the Pea, and the Spider's New Clothes. And it was only after she had told him the story of the Spider and the Seven Dwarfs and had sung him Rudolph the Red Nosed Spider – both of which were his favourites – that he finally went to sleep.

Now things could have gone on forever like this, and Spider George might have remained frightened of people for the rest of his life, had he not run into another George – George the boy.

Spider George had gone off exploring in the garden, and he had found himself by a wall. Now in the wall was a drainpipe. And as George was a curious spider, and as no one had told him not to, he decided to crawl up the drain pipe to investigate, and to see what he might discover.

At first, everything was in darkness, and George became afraid that he might meet something nasty, coming the other way. But then he saw some light, at the far end of the tunnel, and he headed for it, to see what might be there. On he went, climbing upwards, finally to emerge from the top of the pipe into what seemed like a great big empty swimming pool, which had been drained of water.

George looked up then, and just above his head he saw two of the most enormous taps he had ever seen in his life. But he recognised them at once, and he scurried up to have a good look at them, and just as he had expected, one of the taps was marked with the letter H for Hot, and the other was marked with the letter C for Cold. And standing next to the taps, in a huge dish, was the largest cake of soap he had ever come across.

It's a bath! George thought. I'm in the bath. I've come up the plughole. But what sort of creature could have a bath like this? It must be the biggest spider in the world to have a bath this size. It must be the greatest spider ever seen. He went for a walk around. Yes, it must be king of all the spiders! The emperor, even! Or maybe it's a giant spider, as in Incy and the Beanstalk, or maybe –

But then a chilling, terrifying thought came into his head.

– maybe this bath belongs to – a PERSON!

As soon as the thought came into his mind, George leapt down from the side of the bath and made a run for the plughole, so as to get back down the drain pipe, as quickly as he could.

He must have been half way there when he heard a noise.

......................................................................

He glanced up to see the bathroom door opening, but he didn't stop running.

Then he heard a voice, a great booming voice that stopped him in his tracks.

'George –' the voice said, and for a moment George thought that the voice was talking to him. But then he realised that it wasn't talking to him at all. It was talking to a boy who had just come into the bathroom. A boy with the same name as himself.

'George!!' the great voice boomed – at least it sounded like a great voice to a spider, though to a person, it probably sounded quite ordinary. 'Go and get ready for your bath, please. I'll be in to run it in a minute.'

And of course Spider George knew then that the voice belonged to the boy's mother.

He ran as fast as he could to get to the plughole before he was seen. But he wasn't quick enough. A shadow fell over the bath, and George stopped in his tracks, frozen with fear.

This was it.

His worst nightmare.

All his bad dreams come true.

It was –

– a person!

Coming to get him.

George looked up. He saw two big eyes looking down at him. Not nice kind spider's eyes, either. But big, bulgy person's eyes. They may have only been a child's eyes, but they looked big to a spider, just the same.

For a second George was too afraid to move, too afraid to scream. This was it. It was going to happen. The boy was going to pick him up and pull his legs off. This was the end. George braced himself for it.

If only my mum and dad were here to save me, he thought. But he was on his own.

And then, a most curious thing happened. Instead of picking him up and pulling his legs off, the boy just stood there for a moment, frozen, just as George was frozen, and seemingly unable to move.

Then slowly the boy moved his hand, and he pointed at George with his finger, and he uttered the one word.

'Spider!' he said.

And he yelled so loudly that the soap dish fell of the side of the bath.

George was puzzled.

Spider? he thought. Where's the spider? That boy seems to be afraid of a spider somewhere. I wonder where it is? It must be a pretty big spider, to frighten a boy like that.

And George looked around to see where the big spider was, the one that frightened the boy so much, but there was none to be seen.

The boy was yelling very loudly now. And not only was he yelling, he was jumping up and down, and even starting to cry.

'Spider! Spider!' he yelled. 'Mum, Mum! Come quick! There's a spider in the bath!'

Spider George heard footsteps hurrying, and a voice saying. 'Oh, George, not again!' And when he looked up, it was now to see two pairs of bulgy eyeballs looking down at him. There was the big pair and an even bigger pair as well, which seemed to be hidden behind two windows.

Good heavens, thought George. That must be that boy's mother. And look, she's got her own windows! I've never seen a person with their own windows to look out of before. How amazing. Why, if that boy's mother has got windows, then she must be a house. Fancy having a house for your mum. How amazing.

'Spider! Spider!' the boy kept shouting. 'There's a spider in the bath!'

When George heard the boy going on shouting like this, he began to feel rather important.

If I'm so small, and a big chap like that is afraid of me! he thought. I must be more special than I look.

And out of sheer devilment, he puffed himself up to his full size, and he tried to growl and to look fierce, and he showed all this teeth at once, in the hope that he might make the boy even more frightened, and then frighten his mother as well.

'Spider! Spider!' the boy said. 'Nasty spider in the bath!'

But George wasn't able to frighten the boy's mother too.

'Oh, honestly,' she said. 'That's nothing to be afraid of. A tiny little thing like that!'

'It'll run up my trousers,' the boy said. 'And bite me on the bottom.'

'Oh, really, don't be so silly. It's a harmless little spider, that's all.'

Harmless? thought George. Not me. I'm rough and tough and dangerous through and through.

'Kill it!' the boy said. 'Squash it with a newspaper! Pull its legs off!'

'Certainly not,' his mother said. 'I'll put it out of the window.'

Two huge hands descended then. George ran for the plughole. But he wasn't fast enough and the hands were upon him before he could get there.

It really is the end, George thought, It really is. Goodbye cruel world. It was a short life, but a sweet one. It's a pity I never got a chance to grow up, that's all. Good bye Mum, good bye Dad, goodbye all the flies I never ate. I knew it would happen. My worst dream has come true. A person is going to get me!

But to his amazement, the hands neither squashed him nor crushed him nor pulled off his legs. Instead, they very gently scooped him up, and tenderly carried him to the window.

And oddly, George didn't feel afraid.

This person, he thought, isn't afraid of me. And I am not afraid of them. For spiders and people can be friends.

The boy's mother opened the bathroom window, and she dropped George out into the air.

The breeze took him, and he descended on a line of spun silk, and he glided right back down to where he had started. And when he landed, he saw his own mother waiting there for him.

'George,' she said, 'I've been looking for you. I wondered where you had gone.'

George told his mother nothing about his adventures. He kept them to himself as his own personal secret. For children come to an age when they don't want to tell their parents everything, and they wish to have private things for themselves.

His mother did notice something different about him though, and she remarked on it to George's father some days later.

'You know,' she said, 'George seems to have stopped having bad dreams. He hasn't woken up in the night for ages. He doesn't seem to have nightmares any more or worry about people coming to get him. I wonder why that is.'

'It's probably the little chat I had with him,' George's father said. 'It must have put his mind at rest.'

And he felt rather pleased with himself, that he had solved the problem of George's nightmares.

As for George, he slept as soundly as a log. He was no longer afraid of people, and he hoped that they would no longer be afraid of him. But as he got older, sometimes, out of pure mischief, George would creep up on a little girl or a little boy, and he would go 'Boo!' And he would roll his eyes and waggle all his legs at once, and show all of his teeth. And nine times out of ten, the little boy or the little girl would scream and run away, shouting:

'Ahhh! Ahhh! It's a spider!'

And when they did this, George would laugh, and laugh,

and laugh, until the tears ran down his face, and down over his eight hairy legs.

For, to this day, he still can't understand why something as big as a person should be afraid of something as small as a spider.

But it does make him laugh.

And it does make him wonder.

And one thing is for certain – he isn't frightened of people any more.

And he never will be again.

# Desdemona
# Saves the Day

Elizabeth Dale

When Polly saw the parrot in the pet shop, she knew it would change her life. She was beautiful, from her vibrant red crest to her shimmering blue tail feathers. And she fixed Polly with a look that said 'I'm yours!'.

'She's called Desdemona,' said the owner. 'And she's very young. Just the right age for teaching to talk.'

'Oh, Mum, please let's buy her, please?' Polly begged. 'That's what I want for my birthday more than anything. I won't ask for anything else. It's really important to me to have a pet.'

Polly's mum knew that she was thinking of Jet, the dog they'd had to leave behind when they moved into their flat.

'I don't know,' she said, 'Don't you think I have enough to do without a parrot too?'

'I'd clean up after Desdemona. I'd do everything for her!'

'And what about when you get fed up with doing that?'

'I'll never get fed up!' said Polly. 'How could I, when she'd be my friend? Oh Mum, please, I'm so lonely!'

Her mum frowned. Poor Polly was finding it very difficult to settle in to her new home. She hated to see her so unhappy.

'Please!' begged Polly.

'Please!' begged Desdemona and they all laughed.

'We'll think about it,' said her mum.

The first thing Polly heard when she woke on her birthday morning was a loud squawk. She rushed into the lounge and there she was! Her own parrot sitting up high in her golden cage!

'Desdemona!' gasped Polly. 'Oh, Desdemona! Hi there, beautiful!'

'Please?' squawked Desdemona, puffing up her yellow chest.

Polly laughed. 'Oh, you're so gorgeous!' she said. 'I love you!'

'Happy birthday!' cried her mum and dad and her brothers Andy and Steve, rushing in with more presents.

'Thank you! Oh thank you for Desdemona!' cried Polly. 'But I said I didn't want anything else!'

'Just wait and see what it is!' said her mum.

Polly unwrapped a big package of parrot food, a parrot mirror, and a water dish. Right at the bottom was a tiny present, so small it seemed as though it was nothing but paper. In it was a beautiful parrot brooch that looked just like Desdemona!

'Oh, how lovely!' cried Polly. 'I love it. I'll wear it to school. This is the best birthday of my life!'

No one at school knew it was Polly's birthday. But Sally, whom she sat next to, asked her about her brooch and Polly told her.

'Fantastic!' said Sally, 'Are you having a party?'

Polly shook her head. Her mum had asked her if she wanted one, but she had said 'No.' She hadn't really made any friends in her class yet, and she wasn't sure that anyone would want to come.

'Never mind,' said Sally. 'I'd love to see your parrot one day.'

'Perhaps you'd like to come and play after school today?' said Polly. 'That is, if you've got nothing better to do.'

'Brilliant!' said Sally. 'I'll ask my mum, I'm sure she'll say yes.'

She did. And Sally was as entranced by Desdemona as Polly was.

'She's so beautiful!' she gasped.

'I'm going to teach her to talk,' said Polly proudly. 'She's very intelligent.'

'Aren't you lucky!' said Sally. 'Will you bring her into school for Pet Week next term?'

'Try and stop me!' said Polly. 'You'd love to come into school with me, wouldn't you, Desdemona?'

'Please?' said Desdemona.

'Wow!' said Sally. 'She understands you!'

'Of course,' said Polly. 'We have the most wonderful conversations. And she's so polite. What do you say when I bring you your food, Desdemona?'

'Please,' Desdemona said.

'Oh, aren't you clever! Just wait till I tell everyone at school!' said Sally.

'Teatime!' called Polly's mum, bringing in a cake with nine candles on it. It was in the shape of a parrot.

Everyone sang 'Happy Birthday' to Polly. Three times, because the first two were rude versions sung by her brothers.

'That was a little white lie you told Sally about Desdemona, wasn't it, Polly?' asked her mum, when Sally had gone. 'Wonderful conversations, indeed!'

'Just a little one,' said Polly. 'But we will have them, and long before Pet Week. Say please, Desdemona!'

'Happy Birthday!' sang Desdemona. 'Squashed tomatoes and stew!'

'Oh, what a clever bird!' said Polly.

Polly got a book out of the library about teaching parrots to talk. It said to use easy clear sounds, so she started off with 'hello' and 'goodbye' very slowly. Desdemona just looked at her.

'You're not prattling on to that daft bird again, are you?' asked Andy, 'Don't you know it's a bird brain?' He curled up with laughter at his own joke.

'Bird brain!' called Desdemona, looking straight at Andy.

It was Polly's turn to laugh now.

'What did that bird call me!' demanded Andy.

'Bird brain! Bird brain!' cried Desdemona.

'It's got a screw loose!' said Andy, crossly.

'Screw loose!' chanted Desdemona.

'That will teach you to insult my beautiful Desdemona!' said Polly. 'Now then, Desdemona, HELLO. HELLO.'

Desdemona looked at her, unblinking.

'Say it slower!' said Steve. 'It's as thick as two short planks.' He put his nose right up to the cage. 'HELL-O!' he said, very slowly. 'HELL-O! HELL-O! HELL-O!'

'O hell!' said Desdemona. 'O hell! Thick as two short planks! O hell!'

'Steve!' cried their mum. 'What are you teaching that bird to say? Go to your room!'

'Go to your room!' cried Desdemona.

After that, Polly stopped reading the library book, and just chatted to Desdemona, like she would to a friend. She soon realised that Desdemona would pick up whatever words took her fancy, no matter how difficult the sounds were. She also learnt to call people by the phrases they liked to use.

Polly's mum became 'Tidy up that mess!' or 'Cheer up, Polly!', Andy, of course, was 'Bird brain', Polly was 'Hi there, beautiful!' and Steve was something unprintable. And the more words Desdemona learnt the more she used them. Sometimes, it was difficult to get her to be quiet especially when everyone wanted to watch TV.

Polly's dad kept saying, 'Can't we ever have a bit of peace?' So that became Desdemona's name for him.

Soon Desdemona got moved into Polly's bedroom, just so everyone else could carry on with their lives in peace. This arrangement suited Polly, for she was able to have private talks with Desdemona, and tell her about all her problems with trying to fit in at school. Desdemona was a brilliant listener. It was almost as though she really did understand.

'I'm always the last to be picked for teams in games,' Polly moaned. 'I feel so lonely, standing there on my own, the person no one ever wants. I know I'm always going to be last.'

'Poor lonely Polly.' said Desdemona, in a sympathetic voice, nibbling Polly's ear.

'I wish I wasn't so shy,' Polly went on. 'If only I could talk to other people the way I can talk to you, maybe I'd have more friends.'

'Friends?' asked Desdemona, nuzzling Polly's cheek.

'Of course we're friends!' said Polly. 'I don't know what I'd do without you, Desdemona.'

'Teatime!' called her mum.

'Cheer up, Polly!' said Desdemona.

'They're all going to love you when I take you in for Pet Week,' said Polly. 'I can't wait!'

'Can't wait!' agreed Desdemona.

But at long last Pet Week did come. Polly's mum and her brothers helped her carry the cage and stand into school.

'I hope Windbag Windlesham doesn't do one of his great rambling assemblies this morning,' said Andy.

'Wise up! Get real, kid!' cried Desdemona. These were her latest favourite expressions.

'Desdemona is going to have a real eye-opener when she goes into your class,' said Andy. 'They're all batty. What with that screwball Sam, and Snooty Sue Jacks, not to mention that Silly Sally friend of yours!'

'There's nothing wrong with Sally!' said Polly indignantly.

'It's a wonder Bossy Bradshaw's letting you bring Desdemona into school today,' said Steve.

'Miss Bradshaw!' corrected his mum. 'Does she know how noisy Desdemona is, Polly?'

'Oh, I expect she'll be all right,' said Polly. 'With my luck, it'll be so noisy in the classroom that Desdemona won't say a word.'

'Won't say a word!' said Desdemona.

'Now listen here, Desdemona!' said Polly firmly. 'I'm going to die if you don't talk! I've told everyone how clever you are!'

Everyone crowded around the cage as Polly proudly carried it in. They all thought how beautiful Desdemona was, and how quiet, for sure enough, she just looked at everyone without saying a word.

'Doesn't your parrot ever speak?' asked Miss Bradshaw, an hour later.

'Yes,' said Polly. 'She's just getting used to everyone.'

'I don't believe it!' said Sam. 'I think Polly's been making it all up, Miss Bradshaw.'

'Bossy Bradshaw!' squawked Desdemona loudly. The class fell silent as everyone stared at Miss Bradshaw in horror.

'What did she say?' asked Miss Bradshaw.

'Um, Bessy Bradshaw, she's a friend of my mum's,' said Polly quickly.

'Bossy Bradshaw! Bossy Bradshaw!' cried Desdemona. It was too much for the class. They all burst into fits of giggles.

'Be quiet!' cried Miss Bradshaw. 'Be quiet this minute!'

Suddenly, the head walked in, and everyone went quiet.

'There's a lot of noise in here today, Miss Bradshaw,' he said.

Polly held her breath waiting for Desdemona to repeat Miss Bradshaw's nickname, but she didn't. Obviously, even she found Mr Windlesham's glare intimidating.

'It's because Polly's brought her parrot in. They're all a bit over-excited,' said Miss Bradshaw.

'Ah yes!' said Mr Windlesham, walking up to the cage. 'What a pretty bird. Can she talk, Polly?'

'Um, not much, Mr Windlesh ...' As soon as she started to say Mr Windlesham's name, Polly knew it would be a mistake. Especially after what Steve had called him on the way to school.

'Don't be shy, dear,' said Mr Windlesham. 'What kind of things can she say?'

'Windbag Windlesham!' cried Desdemona loudly, right in Mr Windlsham's ear. He jumped and went red. Class 2B burst into fits of laughter. Polly was the only one who wasn't laughing. She just wanted to die.

Just then the bell rang. 'Right, go out to play!' called Miss Bradshaw, with a funny kind of look on her face. It was almost as though she was trying not to laugh.

Polly was the first out of the door. She ran straight out into the playground, as far from Mr Windlesham as possible. The rest of her class followed her.

'Hey, Polly, your parrot's absolutely brilliant!' cried Sam.

'Come and sit with us, Polly,' said Karen. 'You can share my crisps if you like. I want to hear all about Desdemona.'

'Tell us what else she can say!' said Sally. 'I told everyone how brilliant she was, but I didn't think she'd give Mr Windlesham his nickname.'

Polly smiled. Everyone seemed to like her. Perhaps bringing Desdemona to school wasn't going to be such a disaster after all.


After first break, Miss Bradshaw was late back to the classroom. So everyone took their chance to gather round Desdemona's cage.

'You're a pretty bird, aren't you?' said Sally. 'Will you take her out of her cage for us, Polly?'

'Get real, kid!' cried Desdemona, and everyone laughed.

'I don't think I'd better!' said Polly. 'She might get frightened and fly away.

'Oh go on, Polly, stop being such a scaredy-cat!' said Sam. He put his face close to Desdemona's cage. 'You'd like to come out on my shoulder, wouldn't you, birdy-wirdy?'

'Bird brain!' cried Desdemona.

'She says that all the time!' said Polly quickly. 'It's nothing personal, Sam.'

'Sam! Sam! Screwball Sam!' cried Desdemona, repeating what Polly's brothers had said that morning. 'Screwball Sam!'

Sam glared at Polly, as everyone else giggled.

'That's put you in your place!' said Sally. 'Even that parrot knows you've got a screw loose.'

'Screw loose! Screw loose!' called Desdemona and Sam scowled even more.

'It's a lovely parrot,' said Karen, when the laughter had died down. 'You are lucky, Polly. Does she sit on your shoulder? I'd love to see it.'

'Maybe you could come round one night after school?' suggested Polly.

'Oh, yes, thanks! That would be brilliant!' said Karen.

'Of course a parrot isn't as friendly as a dog, or nearly as much fun,' said Sue. 'I mean, you can't take a parrot for a walk or throw bones for it to fetch! And a bird isn't as cuddly or intelligent.'

Polly's face fell. Sue was the most popular girl in the class. She'd been hoping that if she was really impressed with Desdemona, she'd want to be her friend, and then everyone else would too.

'Oh, Sue!' cried Karen. 'How can you say that? Desdemona's gorgeous!'

'Oh Sue!' squawked Desdemona. 'Snooty Sue Jacks! Oh Sue! Snooty Sue Jacks!'

'What did that bird call me?' snapped Sue above the laughter. She rounded on Polly. 'Is that what you call me behind my back? I always said you were conceited and stuck-up. That's why you don't talk to anyone.'

'No!' said Polly. 'Honestly, Sue!'

'Snooty Sue!' cried Desdemona. She loved being the centre of attention, especially when everyone laughed at her.

'I really like you, Sue.' said Polly. 'You tell her, Sally.'

'Silly Sally! Silly Sally! Snooty Sue! Silly Sally!'

Sally stared at Polly, as everyone laughed at her too. She looked terribly hurt. Polly wanted to die, again.

'I've never called you that, honestly, Sally!' cried Polly. 'I wouldn't! It's my daft brothers! They call all my friends names. You know what brothers are like!'

Sally stared angrily at her.

'Silly Sally!' cried Desdemona, and quite a few of the boys in the class copied her, to more laughter.

'She's *your* parrot, isn't she?' said Sally pointedly. '*You* were the one teaching her to talk!'

'What is all this noise?' said Miss Bradshaw walking in. 'Why isn't everyone in their seats reading quietly?' Then she saw Desdemona. 'That parrot has been a right nuisance!' she cried. 'I will not have it disturbing my lessons any longer. Polly Brown, take it away.'

'Yes Miss Brad ...' Polly stopped herself just in time.

'Mad, Brad and dangerous to know!' cried Desdemona.

'Where shall I take her?' Polly asked.

'Anywhere, anywhere as long as it's out of here! Take her to the secretary's office! And cover up the cage. Maybe she'll think it's night-time and go to sleep.'

'Right. I'm very sorry,' said Polly.

'Sorry Polly!' cried Desdemona, as Polly carried her out. 'Wise up and get real, kid! This is serious! So sorry!'

Miss Fordyce, the secretary, lent Polly a cardigan to cover up the cage.

'I hope she isn't too much trouble,' said Polly. 'She's in a very naughty mood today.'

'I'll certainly let you know!' said Miss Fordyce, looking at her severely. 'A bird in my office! I ask you! They're a health hazard! I shan't put up with any nonsense.'

'Oh,' said Polly as she walked out of the door. 'If the headmaster should come in, it might be better if you don't mention his name.'

'What? Mr Windlesham?'

Polly sighed. 'Windbag Windlesham!' squawked Desdemona right on cue from behind the cardigan.

'Desdemona!' cried Polly.

'So sorry!' cried Desdemona, in a voice that sounded anything but sorry.

Polly spent the rest of the day wishing she'd never brought Desdemona to school. She might be popular with some of the naughtiest boys, but Sally wouldn't speak to her and at lunchtime, Sue gathered all her friends around her and whispered in a corner. Polly was sure they were talking about her.

At the end of the day, she went sadly to collect Desdemona. At least Miss Fordyce was out of the office, so she didn't have a chance to moan to Polly.

Polly lifted the cardigan off the cage. Just as she thought, Desdemona was wide awake.

'Hi there, beautiful!' she squawked.

'Just be quiet!' said Polly. 'Don't you dare call anyone any more names!'

'Get real, kid!' cried Desdemona. 'I'll leave the safe unlocked tonight! The keyboards in the music room should fetch £5,000!'

Polly lifted the cage off the stand and went into the entrance hall, where she'd arranged to meet her brothers. But of course they weren't there.

'The burglar alarm switch is under my desk!' said Desdemona. 'The keyboards in the music room should fetch £5,000!'

'Oh do be quiet!' said Polly. 'I've had enough of you today, Desdemona. What's happened to Steve and Andy.'

'What a lovely bird!' exclaimed Mr Cox, the deputy head, coming up to Polly.

Polly jumped. 'Whoops-a-daisy!' cried Desdemona. 'Good luck, George!'

'Um yes, thank you!' said Polly, forcing a smile. 'A bit noisy though.'

'I'll leave the safe unlocked tonight,' said Desdemona. 'The burglar alarm switch is under my desk.'

'What's that she's saying?' asked Mr Cox. 'It sounds as though she's planning a burglary?'

'What?' asked Polly. What trouble was Desdemona landing her in now?

'The keyboards in the music room should fetch £5,000!' said Desdemona. 'I'll leave the safe unlocked tonight. Good luck George! The burglar alarm switch is under my desk.'

Polly stared at Mr Cox in horror. 'I didn't teach her any of that!' she said. 'I'm not planning a burglary!'

'I didn't for a moment think you were,' said Mr Cox. 'All the same, I wonder where she's picked that up from?'

'Miss Fordyce!' gasped Polly. 'She's been in her office all afternoon.'

'And the switch to the burglar alarm is under her desk,' said Mr Cox. 'I think we'd better have a word with the head, don't you?'

'Um, er, no!' cried Polly. 'You see, um, he doesn't like Desdemona, not one bit. I don't think he'd listen to anything she had to say, let alone believe it.'

'Come to think about it, he was saying something about how he hated parrots at lunchtime,' said Mr Cox. 'Let's go to my office, and we'll sort something out.'

Polly thankfully folowed him down the corridor. In the safety of his office, they listened again to what Desdemona had to say.

'She's very good at repeating what she's just heard,' said Polly. 'She doesn't put words together, well, not whole long sentences like that.'

'It sounds to me as though she overheard a phone conversation this afternoon,' said Mr Cox. 'And as Miss Fordyce was saying the safe is being left open tonight, it sounds as though there's a burglary planned for tonight, doesn't it?'

'Wow!' cried Polly.

'Wow!' cried Desdemona.

'Do you think we should call the police?' asked Polly.

'Do you think they'd believe a parrot?' asked Mr Cox.

Polly shook her head.

'Neither do I,' said Mr Cox, 'especially if the head won't. I think the first thing I'd better do is wait here and see if Miss Fordyce really does leave the safe unlocked. You'd better go on home or your mum will be worried.'

'Oh no!' cried Polly. 'I want to stay and see what happens. After all, it was Desdemona who put you on to this. And you never know, she may say something else important while we're waiting.'

'Oh, okay,' said Mr Cox, picking up the phone. 'I'll ring your mum and tell her you're staying on with me because I'm intersted in your parrot, and that I'll bring you home later.'

Perhaps it wasn't going to be such a bad day after all.


Mr Cox and Polly had a long wait, Miss Fordyce stayed in her office typing letters and filing until even Mr Windlesham had gone.

'I think she's waiting until she's last in the school, so no one will notice the safe,' said Mr Cox. 'We'd better switch off the light, so she thinks we're gone.'

'Night night, sleep tight! Make sure the bugs don't bite!' squawked Desdemona, as the light went out.

'Shhh!' cried Polly. 'Night night Desdemona, go to sleep.'

They sat in silence while Miss Fordyce clattering around further down the corridor. Finally, when it was well and truly dark, they heard the sound of her footsteps going down the corridor. Mr Cox and Polly hurried down to her office to check the safe. It was unlocked!

'So the burglary is tonight!' whispered Polly.

'It looks like it.' said Mr Cox. 'I'd better run you home now, out of any danger.'

'But you can't!' cried Polly. 'What if the burglar comes while you're gone?'

'Maybe I'd better ring the police', said Mr Cox. 'Let's go back to the office.'

Just then they heard a van drive into the car park. They rushed to the window to look. It had no lights.

'It's the burglar already!' gasped Polly.

'Stay here!' said Mr Cox. 'I'll go and lock the safe, quick! You watch where he goes!'

Polly stared out of the window. But instead of one man getting out of the car, there were three! And they were heading straight for the front door! What was keeping Mr Cox? They'd catch him if he didn't come back quick!

Polly opened the door to run down the corridor to warn him, but she was too late. The men were just turning the corner. Polly slipped back into Mr Cox's office, while the men walked straight into Miss Fordyce's office – where Mr Cox had just finished locking the safe!

'You just open up that safe again, mate!' said a gruff voice.

Polly could hear the sound of the safe being opened.

'Right!' yelled the same voice 'Out of the way! Don't move, or you're dead!'

'Don't move or you're dead!' yelled an even gruffer voice in Polly's ear, Polly nearly jumped out of her skin. It was Desdemona!

'Who's that?' asked the burglar.

'It's the police,' said Mr Cox. 'They're in my office. They know all about you. And now you're surrounded.'

'You're surrounded!' repeated Desdemona.

'I don't believe it!' said the man. 'How come the only voice is from up the corridor if we're surrounded?!'

Polly opened her cage and Desdemona flew down the corridor.

'You're surrounded' said Desdemona, from outside Miss Fordyce's door. 'You're surrounded!' she repeated from up the corridor. 'Drop those weapons, bird-brains!'

The men dropped their weapons with a clatter. Polly quietly shut the door behind her, picked up Mr Cox's phone and rang the police. 'Come to Mossop Hill School!' she whispered. 'Quick. There's a break in!'

'It's okay now, they're all tied up!' called Mr Cox a minute later.

Polly ran down the corridor, to where the three men sat shamefaced in a corner. They were large, tattooed and unshaven, and she was very glad it wasn't her they'd discovered trying to lock up the safe again. They glared at Polly.

'Where's the police, then?' one of them asked.

'Just checking outside.' said Polly. 'Okay out the back?' she shouted into the corridor.

'Okay out the back!' repeated Desdemona.

There was the sound of police sirens.

'What's that?' asked one of the men.

'Reinforcements!' said Mr Cox.

Polly went out and collected Desdemona and took her back to her cage. 'You clever thing!' she said. 'I forgive you for everything.'

'Everything?' asked Desdemona and nibbled her ear.

'Everything!' said Polly, putting her in her cage.

The police were amazed when Mr Cox told them their story.

'You mean that you and this little girl outwitted three hardened criminals?' exclaimed the sergeant.

'No,' said Mr Cox. 'Me, this big brave girl and Desdemona!'

Polly went and fetched her.

'Drop your weapons!' cried Desdemona. 'You're surrounded!'

Everyone laughed. Everyone, except the burglars.

'Your head teacher will be very impressed with you, little girl,' said the sergeant. 'You've saved the school a lot of money.'

'He'll be very pleased with Desdemona, too,' said Mr Cox. 'Perhaps Mr Windlesham will change his attitude to parrots now, Polly.'

'Windbag Windlesham!' squawked Desdemona. 'Windbag Windlesham! Bossy Bradshaw! Windbag Windlesham!'

'Then again, maybe he won't,' said Mr Cox.

But Mr Windlesham couldn't help but be proud of Desdemona when he heard the news. In assembly the next day he invited Polly up onto the stage with him.

'Thanks to Polly and Desdemona and Mr Cox, this school has been saved from a nasty burglary,' he said. 'What a clever bird you've got, Polly! Have you anything to say?'

'Yes,' said Polly. 'We couldn't have done anything without Desdemona. If she wasn't clever enough to repeat everything she hears, no matter who says it ...' she paused and looked at Miss Bradshaw, Mr Windlesham and in particular Sally and Sue ' ... we wouldn't have known about the burglary or been able to convince the burglars that the school was swarming with police. Desdemona can't help it if people say bad things in front of her. She's the best pet anyone could have.'

'Yes, well, I'm sure we all agree with that!' said Mr Windlesham. 'I think we should all give Polly and her parrot three cheers.'

The whole school stood and cheered her, and Polly smiled proudly.

'I'm sorry I didn't believe you yesterday,' said Sally as they walked back to the classroom. 'Can we be best friends?'

'I want to be best friends too!' said Sue.

'I'll be everyone's friend!' said Polly. 'That's all I ever wanted, to belong.'

'We always thought you were so stuck up!' said Sue. 'You never spoke to any of us.'

'I was too shy,' said Polly. 'And no one knew who I was.'

'Well, the whole school knows who you are now!' said Sally.

Polly smiled. She was right. She could see that everything was going to be different from now on.

# dolphin story collections

## chosen by **Wendy Cooling**